Miss Robinson   5.25

msc

Central and South American Stories

Retold by Robert Hull
Illustrated by Vanessa Cleall
and Claire Robinson

Wayland

Tales From Around The World

African Stories
Central and South American Stories
Egyptian Stories
Greek Stories
Native North American Stories
Norse Stories
Roman Stories
Stories from the British Isles

Series editor: Katie Roden
Series designer: Tracy Gross
Book designer: Mark Whitchurch
Colour artwork by Vanessa Cleall
Black and white artwork by Claire Robinson
Map on page 47 by Peter Bull
Consultant: Chloë Sayer

First published in 1994 by
Wayland (Publishers) Ltd
61 Western Road, Hove
East Sussex BN3 1JD, England

British Library Cataloguing in Publication Data

Hull, Robert
Central and South American Stories.–
(Tales from Around the World Series)
I. Title II. Series
398.2

ISBN 0-7502-1145-8

Typeset by Dorchester Typesetting Group Ltd, England
Printed and bound in Italy by G. Canale & C.S.p.A., Turin

Contents

Introduction

$\mathcal{T}$he story of the first people who settled in Central and South America began perhaps 25,000 years ago. Across from Asia, over the frozen Ice Age sea, came groups of people who wandered south in search of new homelands. By about 10,000 years ago the southern tip of South America, only 1,300 km from Antarctica, was already inhabited. By about 1000 BC there were small towns and religious centres in many parts of Central America.

Every group carried stories on its wanderings. A people's stories told them who they were, where they had come from, how they had been made. Their stories were about everything – stars, animals, music, darkness, words. They 'explained' the world. In one story in this book, music was stolen from the Sun. In another, the rabbit shows why he is cleverer than the jaguar. Another describes why humans don't understand things clearly.

Some of the stories here, like the Inca story of the first city, were only written down many years, or even several centuries, after they were first told. Some peoples, like the Incas, didn't even have writing. But there was no need to write the stories down. They were being told all the time, and memorized effortlessly, and were in no danger of being forgotten.

Luckily for us, these memorable stories haven't faded away. We can hear stories that were first told – some of them – more than 2,000 years ago. We can imagine many settings for their telling: a cool evening in a starlit

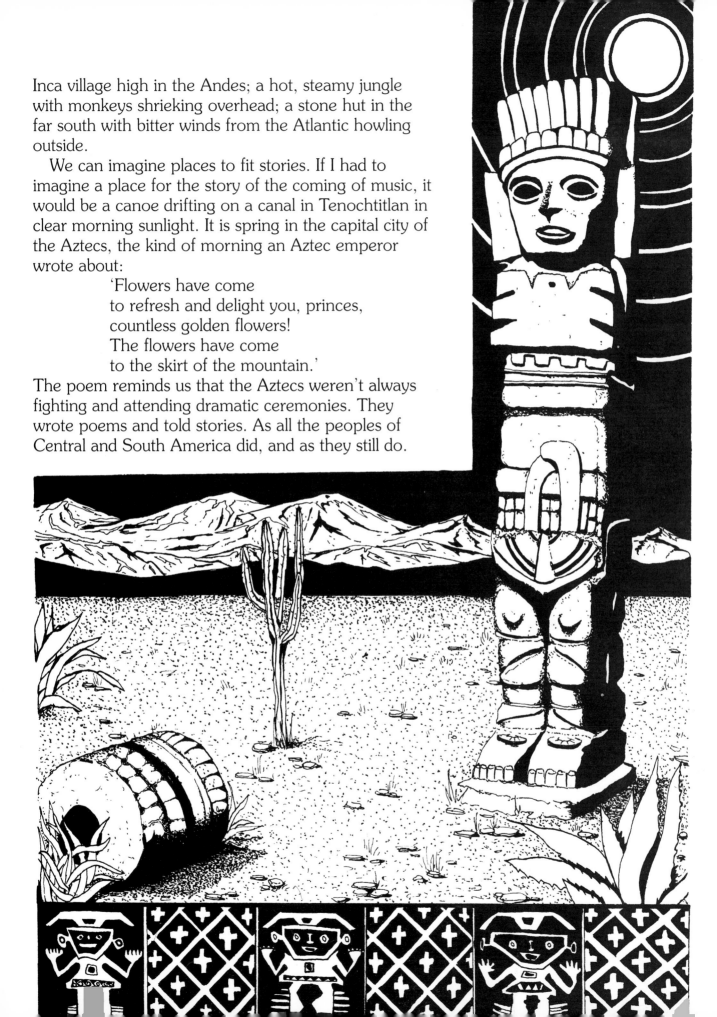

Inca village high in the Andes; a hot, steamy jungle with monkeys shrieking overhead; a stone hut in the far south with bitter winds from the Atlantic howling outside.

We can imagine places to fit stories. If I had to imagine a place for the story of the coming of music, it would be a canoe drifting on a canal in Tenochtitlan in clear morning sunlight. It is spring in the capital city of the Aztecs, the kind of morning an Aztec emperor wrote about:

> 'Flowers have come
> to refresh and delight you, princes,
> countless golden flowers!
> The flowers have come
> to the skirt of the mountain.'

The poem reminds us that the Aztecs weren't always fighting and attending dramatic ceremonies. They wrote poems and told stories. As all the peoples of Central and South America did, and as they still do.

The Beginning of the World

This story comes from the Uitoto people who live in Colombia, a country of jungles, mountains, fertile valleys and sea-coasts in the north-west corner of South America. As in many stories about the beginning of the world, the first thing to come into being is a word.

In the beginning, there was nothing. No time, no space. No desert, no ocean. No eagle, no jungle, no mountain. The darkness was empty, silent, still.

Then a word drifted across the silence. The word was 'father'. A being came from the word 'father' and became the Father, Nai-mu-ena.

Nai-mu-ena was alone amidst darkness and emptiness. He saw nothing, heard nothing, touched nothing. He went on being Nai-mu-ena, alone in the midst of emptiness, for thousands of years.

Nai-mu-ena breathed, he thought words, he dreamed. Once, a gleaming shadow of something swirled across the dark of his dream, like another sudden dream inside the dream he was having. He snatched at this shadow with his mind and caught hold of it.

He kept the gleaming shadow close with him in his mind, thinking and thinking it, so that it stayed there. He was not alone any more. It seemed as if he had made something else to be with him. He breathed and thought, and held on to the shadowy brightness from his dream.

But the glinting shadow that had welled up from the dark of his dreams could not be held or fixed to anything. He could not press it down with a stone, or prop it up with a stick, because nothing existed yet. He had no box or cave to put it in. He was afraid that the shadow might fade away, back into the nothing.

Then he drew out from his thought, like a wisp of raw cotton, the thread of an idea.

He took the word 'Earth' from his thought, and pressed it into the glinting shadow. Then he stood on it, and stamped and stamped on it, like a smith hammering metal. Gradually it took shape beneath him, and spread and spread, until he was able to sit and rest on his dreamed Earth.

Shaped by the stamping of Nai-mu-ena, the bright shadow he had dreamed became the first ground, the floor of Earth. He had dreamed it into being.

Next he made a covering for the ground, raising a roof of sky high above it. He spat into the space between, making clouds, and rains, and forests.

The Earth had begun.

Then he created another being, Rafu-ema, to be possessor of all the stories. Rafu-ema sat in the space under the sky and fashioned this story in his mind, so that we might listen to it here on Earth.

The Songs of the Birds

*I*n many stories, when creatures speak they have different ways of talking. In others, like this one, different creatures share the same language. This story comes from the Kamiaura, one of the Xingu peoples of Brazil. They live near the River Xingu, which flows north for hundreds of miles through the plains and forests of Brazil to the Amazon. The Xingu way of life is threatened nowadays by the building of huge roads, and the destruction of the forests where they live.

Long ago, the birds had no songs. They shared the same language as human beings, and could only speak. All living beings – crabs, crocodiles, trees, flowers – spoke the same language as well. Imagine the first jungle without the howl of monkeys, the snarling of crocodiles at the river's edge, or the endless concerts of bird music.

One day, a young man left his house and went to the edge of the jungle to sit under a tamai tree. He was fed up. He wanted to escape from his dull village, and be someone else, even some other creature.

'I wish I were you, Tamai. I don't like being me. My son does not obey me, and my wife says I'm lazy.'

'You shouldn't want to be me, little son. We tamai trees don't live long. Your friends come and cut our flesh to make bows.'

The young man thought about this for a while. Then he got up and walked on into the jungle. He hadn't gone much further when he saw a column of smoke rising from behind some bushes. He decided to see who lived there. He wanted to talk some more.

When he arrived at the place he found a few of the bird-people burning grass.

'What do you want, father?' they said. They looked surprised.

'Nothing. I was just walking.'

'Sit down then,' the birds said. 'Join us for a talk. We need a rest; we have been clearing a small part of the jungle for our garden.'

The young man sat down, and the birds squatted down next to him. He told them he wanted to be someone else. 'My son does not obey me, and my wife says I'm lazy.'

The birds told him they were anxious about humans, because one had recently been attacking them. He had killed many of the bird-people, they told him: macaws, toucans, eagles, humming-birds.

'What is his name?' the young man asked.

'Avatsiu.'

'Avatsiu! He is from my village! A murderer?!'

The bird-people were pleased at the word the young man used. 'Would you like to come with us back to our village, and be one of us?' They were thinking that he could help them against the murderer Avatsiu.

The young man thought he would like to live amongst the bird-people for a change. He sat for a few minutes thinking, then said he would like to go with them and be one of them.

So off the young man went with the bird-people. They flew on ahead a little way, waiting for him to catch them up. Towards nightfall they arrived at the bird village.

Next day, the chief of the bird-people, an eagle, decided that the young man could wear the feather skin of birds, and be a bird-person. He said that the feathers would have to come from the eagle, because the young man was larger than most of them, and would need wide wings to take him above the Earth. So off the birds flew to the high mountains, to search for long eagle feathers.

By the evening they had returned with enough feathers to make a whole skin. First they spread over

the young man's body a thick white substance, like glue. This was to hold the feathers in place. Then, carefully positioning one feather at a time, they covered him in a coat made entirely of eagle feathers.

'Flap the wings,' said the chief, 'and see if any feathers fall out. It will be a sign.'

The young man lifted the wings and flapped slowly. Not a single one fell.

'Again,' the chief said.

This time, after a few stronger flaps of the wings, a feather fluttered to the ground.

The birds were worried. They spoke in whispers to one another. 'The falling feather is a bad sign. This young man will perhaps not live. Avatsiu will hunt him.'

The next day the bird-people took the man-bird to the place where they trained their young to fly properly. They took him to a high rock, and asked him to look down. He did. He was not dizzy. The chief then asked him, 'Do you see the shelf of rock below?'

'Yes.'

'Do you see the stone lying on the rock?'

'Yes.'

'Well, you are to fly down to the rock and as you swoop across it you must snatch up the stone and bring it back up here.'

The young man was not a coward, but with his wings lifted ready to fall into space, looking down through the empty air that shimmered in the heat over the rocks, he hesitated a moment. Then – over the edge! He felt the upward thrust of the wind under the spread wings, and a fierce tug at his shoulders.

Down towards the rock, down and down, faster and faster, the wind hissing and singing in the feathers!

He missed! He missed not just the stone, but the rock as well, and went hurtling on towards the ground. In a panic, as the ground came up, he struggled to bring his

arms and hands forward. The beating dark wings began to reach round in front of him and slow his fall. But the ground was rushing up to him. It hit his feet and knocked them from under him. He staggered and reeled and fell to a stop in a cloud of dust.

After this, many of the birds were not confident about the young man. 'He cannot fly well enough. He will not be able to help us.'

But others said, 'He will improve quickly. He will be able to aim at Avatsiu and help us snatch him away.'

Next day the birds took him along to Avatsiu's village. They gathered in the trees and on the rocks just outside the village, waiting for Avatsiu to come out of his house. The young man-bird was impatient to try his wings again, and kept lifting them and spreading them out.

Then Avatsiu appeared in the doorway of his house. The man-bird was impatient. He wanted to plunge straight down towards Avatsiu. 'Wait,' the others said, 'wait till he comes right out into the open and stays still.'

Avatsiu made a step into the doorway of his house. It was too much for the young bird-person. Without waiting for a signal from the other birds, he plunged downwards towards Avatsiu.

He missed, and as he had done before he went sprawling in the dust, instead of either landing properly or soaring off to try again.

Avatsiu turned back at the noise, saw the young man-bird, grabbed him, and pulled him inside the house. That was the last the birds saw of him.

Back at their village, the bird-people discussed what should be done next.

'Did the young man have a son?' asked one.

'Why do you ask that question?' another replied.

'Because if he had a son, and if that son knew Avatsiu had killed his father, that son would wish to kill Avatsiu.'

'Ah! Of course!' they said.

'He does have a son,' said one of the birds who had brought him to the village. 'He told us about him.'

The bird-people decided to send a small bird to the young man's son to tell him what had happened. They chose the bright ox-blood bird to give the message. He would be noticed at once, and would be able to lure the son out to talk to him.

The ox-blood bird flew down in front of the house where the dead young man's wife and son lived, and perched on the railing of the terrace. The wife saw the colourful bird, and called her son. 'Look at that bright-coloured bird in front of our house! Look how he puts his head on one side and looks at us, as if he wants to say something!'

The son went outside, and started to stalk up to the bird. The ox-blood bird let him get near, then whispered to him what had happened to his father.

'Do you want to return with me and learn to be a bird-person, and avenge your father's death?'

The son could have said 'yes' straight away, but he wanted to ask his mother's permission. She agreed, and gave her son some advice. 'Do not attack Avatsiu from the front, as your father did. Swoop down on him from behind, then you will be sure to kill him.'

The boy went with the ox-blood bird to the village of the birds. They taught him in the same way they had tried to teach his father, but the son was more skilled as a flier. At his first attempt, he swooped down and took the stone from the rock, and soared back up to the place where the birds waited.

The next day, with the boy-bird as their new ally, the birds flew to Avatsiu's village and gathered in their usual places in the trees and on the rocks in front of the house. 'This is not the right place,' the boy said. 'Wait in the trees behind the house.'

That is what they did, and, when Avatsiu came out, the boy waited until just the right moment and swooped down on to his father's killer. His talons gripped into Avatsiu's shoulder and pulled him along, but he could not lift him into the air with his own unaided strength. Two eagles descended and they too sank their talons into Avatsiu and the three birds soared off towards their own village again.

When they arrived, they killed Avatsiu, because he had killed many of their own people. Then they considered what to do with the body. They decided that, just as he had consumed the flesh and blood of many of their kind, so they would consume the flesh and blood of the killer Avatsiu. The chief of the birds sent two of his people to invite guests from other bird villages to a feast.

Many different bird-people came from the bird villages, and many drank the blood of Avatsiu, the murderer of birds.

Then it happened. As the bird-people drank the blood of Avatsiu their human language left them, and they no longer spoke the same language. Instead, each bird made its own language and spoke that. So, from the blood of Avatsiu came the languages of the birds.

At first some were unsuitable. The humming-bird screamed and the owl murmured. The dove whistled and the kingfisher hooted. When they realized that the languages they had made did not suit them, they exchanged them. The humming-bird and the macaw gave their languages to each other, the kingfisher gave his to the owl, and the owl passed his song to the dove; soon all the bird-people were pleased with their new languages.

They were so pleased that they wished to reward the boy for his help. 'The boy who helped us to avenge the deaths of the birds will return to his home and tell the story of our songs,' said the eagle.

'Yes, and we shall return to our villages, and when the next day breaks, we shall sing,' said the thrush.

'We shall praise the sky with our new languages,' said the warbler.

And they did. And that is how each day has begun ever since.

Why Rabbits Have Long Ears

Rabbits were important in Central American tales. The Aztecs and the Maya drew pictures of the rabbit in the moon, and the rabbit was a symbol of the hunt. And, like the hare in other parts of the world, the rabbit was also thought of as being especially clever. The jaguar, the other animal in this story, was the most feared animal in Central America, and there were many Mayan jaguar gods. So a story in which a rabbit 'tames' and nearly outwits a jaguar must have been fun.

In the early time of the world, different kinds of animals lived in their own separate villages. They didn't quarrel, but visited each other in a friendly way. Sometimes one kind of animal married an animal from another village. New kinds of animals kept appearing, or animals with slight alterations.

They all spoke the same language, too, though in different ways. For instance, monkeys never stopped talking, and it was hard for any other creatures to have a conversation with them (or even for monkeys to have one with each other, for that matter). The sloth spoke about a sentence a month, and it was usually very uninteresting, certainly not worth waiting around for.

But this story isn't about sloths or monkeys. It's about two jaguars, a male jaguar and a female jaguar, and the slightly crazy rabbit who wanted to marry one of them. It's also about how rabbits were given long floppy ears instead of the smart small ears they had in the early times.

14

It all started when one morning there came strolling through the rabbits' village a handsome young jaguar and the beautiful jaguar he was going to marry. The rabbits were hopping about, nibbling and chatting, jumping from one story to another as usual and saying the first thing that came into their heads. And it so happened that the first thing that came into one rabbit's head, as he stopped in mid-nibble to gaze at the beautiful jaguar walking by, was, 'I want to marry her'.

That's what he said aloud. 'I want to marry you, jaguar-lady. You're dazzlingly beautiful, and I'm an unusually clever, fast-talking, ingenious rabbit. We should be happy together and have lots of jaggit or rabbuar children.'

The jaguar friend of the beautiful jaguar-lady, the handsome jaguar she was going to marry, was angry enough to growl a few stern words: 'Hop along, small rabbit-person, and lose yourself in the forest for a long while.' The jaguar-lady just gazed at the tiny rabbit in astonishment.

And the two jaguars walked on, leaving the lovesick rabbit staring after them.

The next day the handsome jaguar was ambling lazily through the rabbits' village again, on his own this time. He was on his way back from the home of his jaguar wife-to-be.

The rabbit saw him, and hopped up alongside. 'About what I said yesterday, Jaguar. I'm serious. I wish to marry her. I may be smaller than you, but I'm faster and cleverer at talking, and probably braver, and a few other things. I have remarkable characteristics. And she looked at me in that special way, too.'

'What special way?'

'The way a beautiful creature would look when attracted by another beautiful creature. She gazed. Perhaps she was impressed by my smart feet, my liquid dark eyes, my exquisite little ears.' The rabbit was hopping about with enthusiasm as he spoke.

The jaguar sat patiently with his tail curled round his front paws and his head on one side.

'I doubt it, somehow. She couldn't believe the rubbish she was hearing, that's all. Now if you'll excuse me . . .'

15

'Wait a minute, wait a minute. When you next visit her why don't you take me with you and we can ask her who she likes best? Or are you scared of competition?'

The jaguar looked down. The rabbit was clever, but not that clever. 'All right, I'll call for you tomorrow morning.'

'Right. Splendid.'

Now, Rabbit really was a cunning animal, whereas the jaguar, though very grand, found that there were many things he didn't understand very well. But he didn't need to. He was so grave and stately, and had such dignified whiskers, that the other creatures all believed he was a deep thinker. All except Rabbit and one or two others, who weren't fooled.

Next morning the rabbit was waiting at the edge of the village, with a little bundle over his shoulder. He had a plan. Along came the jaguar.

'Good morning, Jaguar.'

'Good morning, Rabbit.'

Off they went, Jaguar loping along smoothly, Rabbit hopping and running to keep up. After a while, Rabbit said, 'Jaguar, why don't you let me ride on your back? We could go along quicker. I can hardly keep up.'

The jaguar smiled. Rabbit wasn't very strong, obviously.

'All right, hop up.' And Jaguar crouched low with his belly to the ground, in his hiding position.

Rabbit hopped up and off they went. After a while Rabbit shouted down at Jaguar: 'Jaguar, you go along beautifully fast, but I'm wobbling about. Would you mind if I put this on your back to keep me from falling off?'

As Jaguar looked round to see what 'this' was, he felt something thrown across his back. It was a small saddle.

Jaguar gave a snarly sniff, but said 'Aaarghlll right, if you must.'

Off they went again. After a mile or two, Rabbit said, 'Jaguar, I'm sorry to interrupt, but I can't hold on to your fur properly. I keep slipping backwards. Would you mind if I put this tiny bridle over your head and this ever-so-small bit in your mouth? Then I'd have these little reins to hold on to and we could go along without me interrupting you again.' And out of his bag the rabbit drew a pair of reins and a bridle and bit.

Jaguar growled a small 'hrrrmmm' then said, 'If you're really so weak that you can't hang on to my fur then I suppose I'll wear a bridle and bit. But you won't impress my jaguar-lady very much, needing all this help just to travel a few miles.'

Off again, even faster this time. The bit started to hurt Jaguar's mouth. They were getting near the jaguar-lady's village. 'Faster, faster!' yelled Rabbit. Jaguar suddenly felt a sharp sting near his tail, then another, and a pricking sensation in his side. He couldn't turn round far enough to see what it was, and he didn't seem able to stop.

There were several creatures at the side of the road near the entrance to the village. 'Did I see that or didn't I see it?' a humming-bird said to a macaw.

'You saw it.'

'A rabbit riding a jaguar, a rabbit with reins and a whip.'

'The same. And spurs.'

Jaguar went pounding so hard down the main street of the village that he nearly went past the jaguar-lady's house. He saw it just in time, and pulled up in a great cloud of dust. Rabbit almost went over Jaguar's ears, but fortunately he just held on.

Jaguar-lady came out, and saw her two rivals. With a smirk on his face, Rabbit slid off Jaguar's back and started to dust himself down. The jaguar, who was suddenly ashamed, slunk into the long grass, and flopped down, thinking. Rabbit had been clever.

Rabbit thought he'd been clever, too. He'd completely outwitted his rival.

'You certainly are a clever creature,' the jaguar-lady said. Rabbit flicked his whip at a flower or two, trying to look shy.

'Simple,' he said, 'Brains v. brawn. Always the same result when that happens. But how about you and me? How about the future? Would you be willing to marry me, now you can see who's the cleverest animal-person you know?'

'Well, you'll have to give me time. You're brainy, but there's not much of you. Would it work? Would you be able to bring home a large deer for supper? That kind of thing?'

'If I can ride a jaguar, I can do anything.'

'Perhaps, but hunting takes jaws and teeth. I want my husband to have big snarling jaws, not small chattering jaws. I like jaws that catch supper. Jaws with long, gleaming teeth that terrify all the other creatures.'

Rabbit couldn't help giving a small shudder, but on he went. 'Is it teeth you're after, then, as well as brains? You want a lot, don't you? I'd need to be bigger as well, to carry those jaws about.'

'I promise, if you had teeth as gorgeous as my jaguar friend's, and tried to become a generally bigger sort of rabbit . . . but you can't compete with him as it is. I hope you understand.'

'I understand. I have to find an improved set of mega-teeth and then I would truly be . . .'

'Truly you would,' interrupted the jaguar-lady, without saying exactly what Rabbit 'truly would' be.

'Very well,' said Rabbit. 'I shall go to the Creator-Person, the All-Things-Maker, and make a request.'

Which is what the rabbit did. He went to the Creator-Person, and told him that he needed to have snarling jaws and a mouthful of alarming teeth. And to be bigger. The Creator-Person replied that he could perform some minor alterations, but only with Rabbit's help. Rabbit would have to find two big teeth, one from a giant and one from a monkey.

Off Rabbit went, thinking hard. How could he ever trick such creatures into parting with their teeth? He flopped down and started to nibble thoughtfully on a piece of grass. Suddenly he had an idea – he must have nibbled it. He thought, 'Monkeys like bananas, monkeys like bananas.'

He found some long, thin stones, carved them into banana shapes, and painted them yellow. He scattered them under a tree, and sat and waited. In no time at all a crowd of monkeys came swinging and shrieking down from the tree, grabbed at the stone bananas, and bit them. There were small crunching noises, and bits of teeth flew about. The monkeys stared at the stone bananas, howled and fled. Rabbit hopped out of his hiding place and in amongst the fragments found one whole monkey-tooth.

Next it was the giant's turn. 'How do I lure a giant's tooth out of his mouth?' Rabbit wondered. He ran along the trail to the distant giants' village, hoping for inspiration as he went, but it didn't come. He didn't arrive till it was dark, and the giants were asleep. He sat in the long grass outside a giant's house, gazing at the moon. Suddenly the idea came. Rabbit gave a twisty leap of pure pleasure.

He scampered off into the trees, and came back trailing a long rope of creeper. He made a loop in the end and tiptoed through the dark entrance of a house, pulling the creeper along with him. He found himself in a room where the remains of a fire threw a few flickering shadows round the walls. A steady sound came to his sharp little ears, then he saw the outline of a giant, snoring with his mouth open.

Rabbit peered in and saw the glimmer of a tooth. He slipped the loop over the tooth and ran outside with the other end of the creeper, which he tied to a big tree round the back of the house. Then he went back into the house, picked up some of the embers of the fire, carried them outside and strewed them in the long, dry grass. In a second or two smoke poured from them.

'Fire! Fire!' Rabbit shouted into the entrance of the house. 'Fire! Fire!' There was a muffled roar, then the

19

sound of heavy feet, and the sleepy giant came stumbling out of the hut, waving his arms about. He set off running away from the house. He hadn't gone more than a few yards when he reached the end of his rope. Zoooinggg! It went rigid. The giant seemed to bounce off something invisible, and fell flat on his back. Then, by the light of the moon, a tooth could be seen gleaming at the end of of the rope as Rabbit hauled in his catch.

Rabbit went back to the Creator-Person, carrying the two teeth he had caught.

'Very good,' said Creator-Person. 'You're certainly a clever fellow.'

Then, as he had promised, the Creator-Person gave him a pair of large, powerful teeth. Rabbit felt his mouth go 'ting', and he lifted a paw to his new teeth. They felt long and impressive.

'But what about the rest of me? Isn't the rest of me going to be bigger, to go with my teeth?'

The Creator-Person only laughed. He leaned forward and took hold of the rabbit's neat ears, and gave them a good pull. 'Ow!' Rabbit could feel his ears stretching.

'Have a look at yourself in that puddle of water.'

Rabbit did. His ears were much bigger, but they flopped and hung loose. His teeth, though, looked just right. He turned his head this way and that, lifting his upper lip for a good look. Perfect. Good enough for a jaguar-lady.

Back to her village ran Rabbit, full of confidence. 'Well now. What do you think? I have the finest teeth in the forest, and the most interesting ears. Look.'

The jaguar-lady was sitting with her tail curled round her front paws. It was just after lunch, and she was getting sleepy. She was in the middle of licking a paw,

when who should come along but this ridiculous rabbit-person. She put her paw down and looked at Rabbit. One eye closed a bit, then the other. Ever hopeful, Rabbit thought she was winking at him, but of course she was only getting sleepier by the second.

'Rabbit, you do look' – the jaguar-lady yawned in the middle of her sentence – 'wonderful. You're charming and ambitious. You have fascinating new ears. Your teeth are incomparable. But you're still small, and your improvements are really only' – yawn – 'marginal.' She stretched out, ready to go to sleep.

'Marginal? Marginal? What do you mean?' Rabbit sounded cross.

'I mean' – yawn – 'that they're only minor, they're not really all that important. Now if you'll excuse . . .'

'Not important! Not important!'

But both the jaguar-lady's eyes were closed. She was already dreaming about a certain jaguar.

And that is why rabbits have long ears and long teeth. And why jaguars marry jaguars.

The Coming of Music

*T*he Feathered Serpent, Quetzalcoatl, was the most important god of the early peoples of Mexico. He was wise and kindly, and the inventor of agriculture and writing. Then, in about AD 950, the warlike Toltec people rose to power, conquering many earlier peoples. Quetzalcoatl did not appeal to them as much as their own supreme god, the invincible Tezcatlipoca, 'Smoking Mirror'. Tezcatlipoca was a war god, a wizard and trickster. Quetzalcoatl and Tezcatlipoca became rivals, but they sometimes co-operated, as in this Aztec story.

In the early days of the world, the Earth had no music. Tezcatlipoca, wizard and trickster, and lover of merriment, wanted to have the brightness of music on Earth. He decided he would need the help of Quetzalcoatl, god of all the winds in the sky, even though the two gods were usually enemies. At the beginning of time, with Tezcatlipoca, Quetzalcoatl had lifted the waters of the Earth into the sky to make clouds and rain, and Quetzalcoatl had said that he heard music and dancing near the region of Sun. Tezcatlipoca would ask Quetzalcoatl to go to Sun, and bring music back to Earth.

Hurling his voice up to the clouds, Tezcatlipoca called on Quetzalcoatl. 'Feathered Serpent! Restless wind god, ride here and have speech with me!'

At that moment Quetzalcoatl was drifting quietly above the blue waters of the ocean, which rolled and

whitened under him. Hearing the shouting of Tezcatlipoca echo down from the clouds, Quetzalcoatl hurried over the ocean, whipping up the waves, and soared high above cliffs and mountains, higher than all things that had been made.

He came to Tezcatlipoca. Tezcatlipoca spoke. 'Quetzalcoatl, Earth is sick from silence. We have light and colour, we have rivers and creatures running before our eyes, but we have no music. We must give music to all things, to the rising dawn, to the drifting waters, to the mother with her child. Only in the house of Sun is there music.'

Quetzalcoatl replied, 'I shall go above the blue smoke of Earth into the airy spaces, I shall rise through their boundless sadness to the high house of Sun. He is surrounded by the makers of music, who blow their flutes quietly as they scatter light on to the world. I shall bring some makers of music back to Earth.'

Quetzalcoatl soared into the air, and after many beats of his wide wings reached the still roof of the world. He saw the musicians of Sun, in their different colours. There were musicians in white who sang cradle-songs. In blue there were troubadours, makers of love-songs. There were musicians in red, whose trumpets were for war. And there were flute players dressed in gold, whose songs were the songs of Earth. The gold of their dress and their instruments had been taken from the peaks of the world and milled for them by Sun.

Sun saw Quetzalcoatl hurrying upwards. He knew that the restless wind god of Earth would only have come so far if he wanted something. It must be his music, the music of Sun. Quetzalcoatl must have come to steal the brightly coloured flowers of song. He intended to take prisoner some musicians of gold or blue or white or red, and take them away from the house of heaven.

Sun called out to his musicians, 'Here comes the troublesome wind of Earth. Be silent! Stop your singing! Do not answer when he speaks! He will take whoever answers him and imprison them on Earth. Whoever replies will have to live on Earth in its awful silence.'

24

Listening, the musicians of Sun fell silent.

Quetzalcoatl now stood on the stairways of light in the house of Sun. He hurled his voice upwards: 'Musicians, the supreme gods of Earth call to you. Come with me, and bring your music to Earth. Sing the Earth. Sing its dawn for us, its rivers and mountains, its jaguars and turtles and macaws.'

Quetzalcoatl hovered on his dark wings, waiting. But no voice answered. Quetzalcoatl shouted again. 'Come, musicians. Sing a new song in the forests of Earth. Leave the blinding flame of Sun, and sing the freshness of the grass and the cool streams.'

There was no answer. Quetzalcoatl grew angry. He would storm Sun. He whipped up black clouds, and threw lightning across them. He piled the clouds higher and higher till they seemed to threaten Sun. He let loose the shattering voices of his thunders. The noise rocked the heavens from end to end, and the frightened musicians fled this way and that, thinking that the house of Sun was falling. Some of them fled to Quetzalcoatl; they were enough for his purposes. He put an end to the dark turmoil in the sky, and, taking the group of musicians on his huge wings, glided down towards Earth.

The return of Quetzalcoatl was seen everywhere. The face of Earth shone, seeing him descend. The lakes and rivers glittered a greeting; everything welcomed Quetzalcoatl returning to Earth with the precious stolen music. Everything greeted the wind god, the breath of Earth returning with music from Sun. The awakened voices of the people greeted him, and so did the wings of the quetzal bird, the faces of the flowers, and the red cheeks of the fruit.

Sun's musicians spread to the four corners of the world. Quetzalcoatl himself sang. His voice went drifting along the valleys, through the forests and over the sea.

That is how music came to Earth.

25

The First Inca City

The people known as the Incas settled high in the Andes mountains in about AD 1100. Over the next two or three hundred years, they built up an empire that stretched 5,000 km along the coast and mountain regions of South America, north and south of their great capital, Cuzco, a city of 200,000 people. The name 'Inca' was given to them by the Spanish, because their emperor was called 'Sapa Inca'. This legend describes how the children of the Sun, the first Inca rulers, founded the first city.

When Inti, the Creator and sun god, made people, he was pleased with his work. These humans were handsome and thoughtful, and could make things. Then, after a while, Inti became less satisfied. The people he had made were too much like wild animals. They lived in caves, and their clothes were of bark and animal skin. They ate only berries and roots. They had no laws. They had not learned to make silver or gold ornaments. They did not even worship their own maker.

It was time to help them. He would send two of his children, his son Ayar Manco and his daughter Mama Ocllo, to show people better ways of living.

He called them to him. 'Tomorrow at dawn you will go down to Earth. The people live like animals, and must be taught how to be proper human beings. You must show them how to come together and live in villages, how to grow plants and make animals obey.

'You must pull fibres from trees and the backs of animals and weave wool and cotton. After that, make tools and hammer metal, and tell the people to watch you. Carve stones for them, and cut jewels. Make the people follow your movements. Then tell them how to speak rules and laws, and give some of the people the task of remembering them. Lastly, tell them who they are, and who their maker is, and instruct them in ways of praising me.'

Ayar Manco and Mama Ocllo replied, 'We shall do as you say, Father, though we shall be sad to leave our home in the sky for Earth.'

'Earth is beautiful, and it will be your work to make it more so. But there is one more thing I must say. Before you can do the things I have asked, you must settle somewhere. You must be in one place. A city waits for you to found it. You will discover the place with the help of this.'

Inti drew from his robe a long spike of gold. 'After you arrive on Earth and begin your wandering, whenever you pause to rest or eat or sleep, try to drive this spike of gold into the ground. The ground will resist, again and again. But there will come a moment when the gold spike sinks easily into the ground, and disappears. That is where you will build your city, and teach the people.'

At dawn, the two children of the Creator, dressed in dazzling white robes ornamented with gold, rode the beams of the rising Sun down to Earth. They came to the edge of a still lake just as the Sun's light kindled the mountaintops.

Some people were crouching near the water, gnawing roots. They cowered back in terror when they saw Ayar Manco and Mama Ocllo striding towards them like the Sun's light over the rocks. But after the children of the Sun had walked past them, the people realized they were gods and could not help following them.

So began a long journey through the mountains. Ayar Manco and Mama Ocllo walked steadily on, followed by more and more people, all of them as curious as the first few. Wherever they stopped, Ayar Manco and Mama Ocllo lifted the golden spike high over

28

their heads, and tried to drive it into the ground. Time and time again the ground resisted, and on they went.

One morning, after travelling for many days, they reached a narrow plain with high mountains on all sides. In the ground of this green, beautiful valley the golden spike sank easily and buried itself.

Ayar Manco spoke. 'This is to be the site of the first city of the Inca family, the children of the Sun. The city will be called Cuzco.'

Mama Ocllo said, 'We must explain what we intend to the people who have followed us. Before they can help us build a city, the people have to know what to do.'

The two children of Inti stood in their shining robes before their people, and gave them instructions. They showed them how to cut wood and shape stone, to make steps of wood to climb with, to build walls with stones fitting so closely that no shaking of the ground could topple them. Ayar Manco and Mama Ocllo taught the people how to choose seed and grow grain, and how to make hoes and dig channels to carry water from field to field. They showed them how to keep llamas in stone pens.

It was time to begin building the first city of the Incas, in the valley high in the mountains. The people went to fell timber, and went out on the rocky hillsides to cut stone. Soon they had made a road to walk on, and a few houses.

But in this valley an immense wind howled amongst the rocks and flattened the grass. The Sun could hardly hold its course across the sky, and when the people carried timber, the wind tore it from their shoulders and sent it spinning through the air. It clawed huge stones out of their arms and bounced them down the mountainsides. Sometimes Ayar Manco and Mama Ocllo and the people could only watch in dismay as huge boulders sailed across the hillsides like bubbles over a stream and tall trees went spinning through the air like bits of straw.

What was to be done? Ayar Manco and Mama Ocllo knew that they had to trick the wind. They watched it racing up the rocky slopes, hurling clouds of dust into the air. It was like a wild creature, so why not trap it?

29

Ayar Manco and Mama Ocllo built a great stone pen, like those they had taught the people to build for the llamas.

Ayar Manco and Mama Ocllo waited for the wind to come down from the mountain. They heard it thumping above them between the valley walls, then saw it racing amongst the houses, twisting its column of dust as it ran. It ran straight through the great gate of the pen. Ayar Manco and Mama Ocllo slammed the gate. They had penned the wind. In anger it howled and shrieked round the stone enclosure, but it was trapped.

Now that Ayar Manco and Mama Ocllo had lured the wind into prison, the people could get on with their work without being harrassed and pushed about. The stones that they carried rested steadily in their arms. The wood they shaped wasn't grabbed and flung out of their reach.

The building went on peacefully for a time. Then another of Inti's children, Ayar

Manco's brother, Ucho, arrived from his home in the plains. There the wind was quiet, and a great friend of Ucho's. If the wind were imprisoned and its friend Ucho did not help, it might take a terrible revenge on the people of the plains.

When Ucho heard the din that came from the pen where his friend thrashed about and howled, he insisted that the wind should be set free. 'The noise of his pain is unbearable,' he said.

He threatened that if Ayar Manco and Mama Ocllo did not do this he would do it himself. He said he would release the wind that very day, at sunset. Ayar Manco and Mama Ocllo were appalled. If the wind ran free again they would never complete their work. The people would never be able to carry stones to the top of the temple. The timber pointing upwards, waiting to support the roofs of the houses, would be snatched away and hurled to the valley floor. The first city would stand unfinished.

Ayar Manco gazed up towards the Sun. It was climbing along the steep side of the mountain on one side of the valley. It would rise for a while longer, reach the summit, and then begin to drop towards the mountain on the opposite side. They had only a few hours to finish the city.

Unless . . . unless . . . As Ayar Manco gazed, an enormous idea came to him. He would stop the Sun in its course. He had penned the wind. He would tether the Sun.

Ayar Manco made a long gold chain. Throwing its heavy loops over his shoulder, and taking a few of his strongest servants with him, he climbed the mountain. The Sun was almost at the summit. They waited for a few minutes till the Sun passed close over them, then Ayar Manco and his servants hurled the chain out over it. The chain fell and dangled glittering in the sky, far out over the mountainside. Ayar Manco ran and took the loose end of the chain, and with his servants wound it round a tall rock. The Sun could not go any further across the sky. There would be no sunset until the city was finished.

The light of the Sun stayed bright, the air was still. The echoes of axes on wood and hammers ringing on stone floated across the valley endlessly, hour after hour in the long day that never ended. The people slept in the shade when they were tired, and woke in the same light and started again. Soon the houses had roofs, and the topmost stones of the temple were laid. Soon Ayar Manco and Mama Ocllo were able to look round their city, the city of their people, and know that it was finally built. They were satisfied. It would be a good city.

Mama Ocllo opened the gate of the pen that imprisoned the wind, and it fled howling past her up the mountain and over into the next valley.

Then Ayar Manco looked up towards the top of the mountain, to the hitching-post of the Sun. He climbed again, and set it free.

Night came, and next day the Sun rose as usual. As usual, the wind poured through the valley and over the mountains. But the Incas had built their first city.

31

Making Humans

The Maya peoples lived in several areas of Central America, to the south of the Aztecs in Mexico. Their civilization flourished between about AD 300 and 900. Eventually their towns decayed, and their huge pyramid temples lay hidden in the jungle until the nineteenth century. They had amazingly accurate calendars and a writing system, but their stories have also been passed down by word of mouth for over a thousand years. This one, about the first humans, comes from the *Popul Vuh*, or *Sacred Book of Advice*.

In the early days of the world, there was nothing but darkness – dark, empty sky and dark, motionless water. In the depths of the water drifted Tepeu, the Creator, and Gucumatz, the Giver of Form. They lay in the cold silence, wrapped in the brilliant feathers of the precious quetzal bird.

A thought came to the gods. It spoke to them, and they spoke the words aloud: 'Brightness will come.' They spoke the words again, and again, and watched. They gazed into the dark, waiting for the effect of their words.

'Brightness will come,' they said again. Then the morning star was born, and the Sun. Tepeu, the Creator, and Gucumatz, the Giver of Form, gazed into the first dawn. The world whitened with light and the sea shone for the first time.

Next the gods thought about the shape of the world. They wanted to make Earth. 'Before Earth, there is water to be poured away and got rid of,' they thought. 'Then Earth will need to be shaped and levelled and planted.'

So the gods poured away the unwanted waters and asked the mountains to rise in the spaces where they had been. They trod paths for the rivers amongst the mountains, and drew cloud round the high summits. They shaped fields and made valleys.

Then they thought of the creatures they could bring there. They spoke the names of many creatures, and with the name 'deer', deer came to the forest, and with 'panthers', panthers, and in the same way jaguars came, and ocelots, and eagles, and parrots, and monkeys, and many more.

And the Creator and Giver of Form distributed homes amongst the creatures. 'Parrots, you make your homes on the branches of the trees. Eagle, you take the clifftop for your house. Crocodile, you take the river.'

Then they thought, 'Should the world remain silent? Should there not be voices and sound?' And they gave to the beaches the crash of waves, to the trees the whisper of leaves. They gave small splashing noises to the springs dripping from the rock, and a murmur to the air.

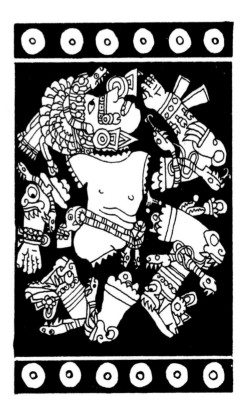

Then they said to the animals and the birds, 'Talk now. Speak to each other, and praise your Makers. Praise Tepeu, the Creator, Gucumatz, the Giver of Form, and all the gods. Sing hymns of thanks.'

The creatures began to make noise, and the forest was filled with the swelling chorus. But the noises were not talk. No words of praise were spoken or sung to the gods. There was only a wordless din, the howling of monkeys, the hiss of snakes, the scream of macaws. There was rattle, croak, growl and screech, but no song of praise or worship.

The gods had failed. 'It is not good,' they said. 'We have not arranged it so that they can talk. The world is not successful.' So they decided that the creatures they had made would not have great power. They would eat each other, and be servants of any better being who praised the gods in words.

Tepeu and Gucumatz thought, 'We will begin again. We will make a being to praise the gods, a being who will be ready with gratitude.'

So the gods began to make the first human. They took earth and mud, and made a body. They moulded it and stood it erect. But it didn't work. It was damp and soggy, and kept slipping down and coming apart. The creature's head wasn't round; its face had only one side. It made no sense when it tried to talk, and its eyes couldn't be looked into.

'It can't even walk,' Tepeu said to Gucumatz. 'Its mind is dark.' So they threw away their first attempt, and started again.

'What else can we try?' Gucumatz asked. 'We must look around, and find another way.' And they found wood, and thought that they would make humans from that. The gods could easily form beings of wood, just as they hammered gold rings and cut gems for their own pleasure. They started to carve a broken tree, and soon a shape began to form. 'It is turning out well, this shape. There is movement in its stillness. There is the wind's breath inside it, flowing through it, as it flowed along the living branch.'

Soon one wood-man breathed, and spoke. He talked words. Then he walked. The gods made another, and another. And so the race of wood-people came into being. They married, and multiplied, and spread round the world.

But the gods were not satisfied. The wood-people had no hearts or minds. They were dry people. They had no sweat, or fat, or blood. They jerked along like dolls and did not think. They were so thoughtless that their chickens and dogs complained, and said, 'You give us nothing. You sit eating and lecturing us and give us nothing but kicks under the table.' The wood-people's pots and plates and griddles and grindstones joined in. 'You allow us to become black and sooty, you drop us on the floor and shatter us, you gouge and scratch and scrape us.'

So the dogs and chickens said, 'Now we are going to eat you back.' And they ran after the wood-people and chased them. Then the pots and plates and griddles and grindstones hurled themselves at their owners and

tried to bang their heads and shatter their limbs. The wood-people started to run away, but when they climbed over the roofs to escape, the stones in the walls of the houses decided to fall and throw them down to the ground, so many of them splintered and broke. The world was against the wood-people.

No word of thanks or praise ever came from the wood-people, so Tepeu and Gucumatz joined in with the pots and plates and stones, and the dogs and chickens. Over the places where the wood-people ran to, they sent daytime rain and night-time rain, again and again, a long, dark rain. A great flood washed the wood-people away, except for a few, who ran to the forest and became monkeys.

The gods had to begin again. They would make people from something that lived, something firmer than mud but less

dry than wood. But what? They puzzled and waited. Then there came flying to them a parakeet and a crow. They were carrying yellow and white ears of corn. The gods had created so much that they had not had time to see all they had made, and they had not seen corn before. It was as if the birds had brought it to them as a sign. Then a wildcat came running, and soon after a coyote, and together they led the gods to where the corn was growing.

The animals pointed out the road to Tepeu and Gucumatz, and they followed it. They took the yellow corn and the white corn, and shaped four bodies from them. They gave them names. These looked like the men and women the gods had wanted. They became men and women. They breathed and existed. They had fine faces. They looked round them. They saw and heard. They walked. They spoke.

The gods had made the first humans. They watched them. They watched them seeing the world. They talked to them, asking question after question: 'Can you see well? Is your life pleasant? Do you enjoy your walking? Aren't the mountains clear? Isn't your language fine? Listen to the rivers! Look at the eagle circling!'

But Tepeu and Gucumatz could see without waiting for their answers that the people saw clearly, and that they saw everything. Their gaze passed over mountains and lakes and rivers. They spoke splendid thanks for having been made: 'Truly we give you thanks for making us. We thank you for our mouths and faces. We see, we hear. We dream and think. Our understanding is great. Our thanks to you that we are created. Our thanks to you that we exist, that we have been shaped and formed.'

The gods looked at the four humans and thought again. 'Their sight reaches into everything. They see all the Earth and the heavens. They understand all that they see. This is not good. Their understanding reaches too far. They will be like gods. We shall need to do something more, so that they are not equal to us. We shall have to unmake them a little.'

So, because the first men and women were too wise and saw as much as the gods, Tepeu and Gucumatz blinded them a little. They chipped the clear surface of their gaze. They clouded the mirror of their understanding so that they would never see clearly. In that way, men and women lost their understanding from the start. From the very beginning they could not see the world properly. Though the mountains rose sharp and clear and the water shone, whatever the first four looked at they saw dimly, as if they were looking into a mirror of dark obsidian.

Then when the gods brought them beautiful wives and husbands, and beautiful children, their understanding was dim, too. And so it has always been since then.

Star-Girl

A farmer came to live in a village in the mountains. His sons and daughters and new neighbours helped him make a field. They built a stone terrace that would prevent the land from slipping down the hillside, and they carried rich soil from the valley and spread it over the thin earth. Then they dug a little canal to bring water to the field.

The farmer wondered what to grow. On the other side of the valley there were many kinds of crops – potatoes, tobacco, maize, beans. He decided to plant potatoes.

The farmer worked from dawn till sunset planting his field, weeding between the rows he had made, hoeing and watering the soil. Every evening he would look out from his house and gaze across the valley at his field. The fresh soil gleamed under the moon, and the stars seemed to lean down for a closer look.

His field was soon full of young potato plants, waving their flowered white heads in the breeze. The farmer thought of the thousands of delicious small white potatoes hiding below the surface of the soil, growing bigger every day.

He waited and waited, then one morning he decided the potatoes must be ready to eat. He thought, 'Tomorrow I shall start to dig them up.'

Soon after dawn, while the misty-headed Sun hauled itself slowly up the opposite mountain, he strode off to pull up potatoes and reap the reward of all his hard work.

The track went down into the village, then turned upwards past other terraced fields. As he walked the farmer thought of nothing but the pleasure of digging up glistening new potatoes. He came to the last corner, and looked over the stone terrace wall. He was filled with dismay. All over the field, plant after plant had been pulled up and thrown aside, their potatoes taken!

He spent the day digging up some of the potatoes that were left, wondering who the thief could be. No one in the village was hungry, and he could think of no enemies who would do it – he had not lived there long enough to make enemies. It must have been a group of hungry, homeless wanderers. His anger died down, and he decided not to worry over a few stolen potatoes. He could replant the parts of the field that had been robbed.

But the next day the same thing happened. He came to his field at dawn to find that the thieves had come in the night again and taken more of the ripest potatoes.

And so it went on, night after night, until there were hardly any potatoes left. In the end, the farmer told his eldest son to keep watch in the field at night.

The young man took some warm blankets and went up to the field at nightfall. He lay down at the edge of the field. It was a cold, misty night, and he pulled his blankets close round him, and almost dropped off to sleep.

He was roused by thin rustling noises. He lifted his head over the edge of his blanket and saw lights moving mistily over the field. Silvery light leapt and slid across his eyes, like reflections in dark water.

He lay still and watched. Were his eyes telling him the truth? The thieves of his father's potatoes seemed to be beautiful girls and young women, whose robes rustled as they bent to the ground to fill their silver baskets. They hummed and sang and talked as they worked. Their arms and hair, their robes and jewelled clasps and rings shone like stars. The field was flooded with starlight.

The young man nearly forgot about potatoes. He gazed at the beautiful star-women, admiring their graceful movements as they uprooted the plants, shook off the earth and dropped the potatoes in their bags. It

40

might be worth losing a few potatoes, he thought, for such a vision. But as he gazed at them he realized that his father would hardly believe him if he said that star-girls were stealing his potatoes. He could almost hear him: 'Star-girls stealing my potatoes! Moon-brain! Mist-head! Another of your mountain dreams!'

Perhaps it was. There was one way of finding out. He leapt out from his hiding place and ran towards a star-girl. 'Potato thief!' he cried. He snatched at her arm and held her. She screamed.

He felt terrible. 'I'm sorry,' he said, 'I hate having to hold on to you when you are screaming like that, but you are a thief; those are my father's potatoes in your bag.'

'Let me go! Let me go!' she screamed again. When the rest of the star-girls heard her and saw the young man holding on to her, they cried in alarm and flew up like a flock of white birds into the night sky.

The young man held on tightly to the beautiful thief he had caught. He slackened his grip on her arm and took her white hand, tying it loosely to his with a length of twine. She calmed down a little, and after a few quiet minutes of gazing at her, he didn't know what to think. Should he treat her as a thief? Or was she just a beautiful woman he'd found and caught? Should he take her to his father? Or keep her in a secret place?

He decided not to make up his mind at once, so for a few days the star-girl was prisoner in a stone hut on the mountainside. She kept crying and pleading with him, 'Let me go, let me go back to the sky!' The more she pleaded the more he wanted to keep her. But he could not keep her in the hut against her will. He decided to ask his mother's advice.

One night, he took her down to the village and hid her in a room in his house. In the morning, after his father had gone to the fields, he took her to see his mother. She was overjoyed to see him, and astonished at the beauty of the star-girl, who shed light and radiance round the room. His mother agreed to keep the star-girl in her house, if she became her son's wife, and if her husband agreed.

When the young man's father came home he was amazed to find that his son had brought home a young

woman whom he wanted to keep as his wife. He was even more amazed when he heard who had been stealing his potatoes.

'Don't make me live here,' the star-girl cried tearfully. 'Earth is not my home. The sky is my home. I will go home and bring back all that we stole from you, I promise. I'm sorry we took your potatoes, truly sorry. Forgive me.'

But they ignored her pleading. 'You can keep her, son,' the farmer said, 'She can live with us.'

Though the farmer let his son keep the star-girl as his wife, he said that she would have to stay in the hut until dark every day, and have to wear ordinary clothes. Her shining hair would need to be covered, too. Otherwise people might wonder who she was.

The star-girl's silver clothes were folded and hidden away. She was given dull human clothes, and her shining hair was tucked out of sight under a drab shawl. She became the young man's wife, and a prisoner on Earth.

So the star-girl stayed with the family, and even her unhappy presence seemed to bring light to the house. The farmer and his wife grew fond of her and made a fuss of her. But Earth would not become her home. She could not get used to treading on the ground, being touched by human beings and surrounded by echoey, dark rooms and noisy, smelly creatures. After dark she would stand outside the house, to gaze up at the stars and weep. She remembered looking down from a great height on snowy mountains and glinting lakes, and being surrounded by whispering empty skies or hurrying clouds. Every day she grew sadder and more silent. She was stifled in her dark, heavy clothes, and desperate to go home.

She was so miserable that one day the young man's mother asked her what was wrong. Was there anything, she asked, that might bring a smile to her face and make her talk, even if it was only for a little while?

'I would like to let my hair fall free and be allowed to wear my own star clothes,' she said, 'even if it is only for an hour or two. Just to remember what I once was, and the kind of life I had.'

At first the young man and his mother and father refused, but day after day she became more miserable and tearful. Finally they gave in and said that for one evening she could wear her star-garments.

As soon as she had put them on, she became a radiant being again. Her true self shone brightly in her face and from deep in her heart. 'Let me stand outside and look at the stars,' she said. 'Just for a minute or two.'

The young man took pity on her. 'Well, just for a minute or two,' he said, and opened the door for her.

She stepped outside in her star-dress and looked up above the mountaintops. Then she turned to look at the young man. The light of the stars shone from her eyes and dazzled him. He put his hand up over his eyes. When he looked again she had gone. A freezing wind blew suddenly through the doorway. He looked out and saw a faint white shape swirling above the house, like an ember from a fire. She had gone.

As the days went by the young man grew desperate for her. Every night he climbed the mountain to be near the stars, and stood looking up through the clouds, hoping to see her. He whispered his thoughts aloud to the dark sky, and even imagined, in the cold breeze swirling round the rocky summit, that he could hear a silvery voice whispering replies.

But he saw no one; no star-girl with silver arms and hands came to console him. She was too far away above him, and finally he gave up going to the mountaintop, and brooded alone in the fields. One morning, when he was deep in

a black despair, a shadow swooped across the field. A condor's shadow. He looked up and watched the great bird circling and circling, rising in the warm air towards the mountaintops. Condor, he thought, could fly on his wide wings higher than any mountain. Condor could rise to the sky. Condor could take the young man to the stars.

Next day the young man climbed the mountain to find the condor, and out of pity for his distress the great bird agreed to carry him on his broad wings up to the stars. But he said that the journey was long and tiring. The young man would have to sacrifice two llamas for food, one to build up the condor's strength before they left and another to eat on the way.

The farmer and his wife tried to persuade their son not to attempt the perilous journey, but the young man would not listen. He wanted to find his wife. He could think of nothing else.

The young man killed two llamas and dragged them up the mountainside to the condor's home. The condor devoured the first in no time, and then said he was ready. He told the young man to climb on to his wings with the other slaughtered llama. 'Keep your eyes closed during our flight,' he said, 'and when I say "meat", cut me a piece from the second carcass and feed me that. But do not open your eyes.'

And the condor launched himself out into the warm mountain air with the young man on his back holding the slaughtered llama. With his eyes shut tight, the young man could hear the hissing flow of the air over the feathers and feel the beat of the surging wings. After a while he heard the condor cry 'Meat', and he reached down and fed him a piece. And so they went on, higher and higher, into colder and colder skies. The young man fed the condor until there was hardly any food left. Then the last piece of carcass was gone. They had still not arrived and the condor's wings were beating less strongly. 'Meat!' The young man bent and cut flesh from his own leg. The wings surged again. Three times the young man had to feed the condor with meat cut from his own body.

Then the young man felt the condor's feet touch the ground. He opened his eyes. They had landed in the sky-world, next to a glittering lake. Both of them were exhausted and dirty. The condor looked bedraggled and old, but when he had bathed in the lake he looked almost as he had done when they left Earth. The young man bathed too, seeing from his reflection in the water that on the long journey he had lost some of his youth. He needed the lake's magic waters to bring most of it back.

'Over there, look!' The condor was pointing to a temple at the far end of the lake. Twenty or thirty young women, dressed in the same robes the young man had seen in the potato field, were performing a stately dance along the shores of the lake. 'A ceremony will soon begin in the temple,' the condor said. 'Go across to it and wait in the doorway. When they finish their dance they will walk past you into the temple. They will all look the same to you, but if your wife is amongst them she will brush against you as she passes. That is all the recognition she will give. The others must not see that she knows a man from Earth.'

The young man obeyed the condor's instructions. Sure enough, he did not recognize his wife's face

45

amongst those passing by. Then one of the star-women brushed against him as she went into the temple.

The young man was overjoyed, but what did it mean? He ran back to the other side of the lake where the condor was waiting for him. 'What shall I do next, Condor?' he said.

'Wait again at the entrance. As she comes out from the temple she will give some signal to you. Follow her. After that your fate is in her hands.'

The young man waited again. As the condor had said, she made a signal to him as she came out, this time smiling and whispering for him to follow her. The young man's heart leapt with hope and longing.

A little way beyond the temple, she turned to him. 'I know that you love me, enduring such a journey and waiting so long for me. But it is not to be. I cannot keep you here, and I cannot go back with you to Earth. There is no hope for love between a star-being and an Earth-being. There never was. Do you not realize that? Now I must go. I shall always remember you. Go now. Go back to Earth, to the mountain and the village with its terraces and potato fields. They are not for me, and the sky is not for you.'

And she turned and left him. He knew he would never see her again.

The condor carried the young man back to Earth. Gliding down slowly from the sky-world, they arrived at the village early one morning, as the sun began to creep over the slopes of the terraced fields. The young man's father and mother had given up hope of ever seeing him again, and the day of his return was the happiest of their lives. When he told them that his wife would not return from the sky-world with him, they were sorry, but told him not to dwell on the past. They said he should look for a new wife amongst the girls of the village.

But the young man had no interest in looking for anyone else. His true and only wife was the star-girl he would never see again. Instead of marrying and raising a family, he became a thoughtful, sad man, old before his time, who at night used to climb the mountain just to gaze at the stars.

Notes

Aztec (p. 5, 14, 21, 32)
The word 'Aztec' probably comes from the word 'Aztlan', meaning 'the place of cranes'. Aztlan was the lake alongside which the Mexica people, the main group of Aztecs, were supposed to have once lived. After two centuries of wandering the Mexica founded Tenochtitlan on an island on Lake Texcoco, and started to extend their power over other groups who lived round the lake. All of them, the Mexica and the peoples they had power over, were later called Aztec.

Ayar Manco (say Ah'-yah Mahn'-koh) (p. 26-31)
A son of Inti, the Inca sun god. With his sister, Mama Ocllo, he founded the first Inca city.

Gucumatz (say Goo-koo-mahts') (p. 32-8)
A Maya god of creation. His name means 'Giver of Form'.

Incas (p. 4, 26, 29, 31)
In the fifteenth century the Incas had an empire that extended 5,000 km along the coast of South America. They had no writing system, but they were brilliant engineers and builders. The emperor of the Incas was supposed to be descended directly from the Sun.

Inti (say In'-tee) (p. 26, 27)
The Inca sun god. His children, Ayar Manco and Mama Ocllo, became the first Incas.

Mama Ocllo (say Mah'-mah Oh-kloh') (p. 26-31)
A daughter of Inti.

Maya (p. 14, 32)
The Maya peoples lived to the south and east of the Aztec empire, in Yucatan, Belize, Guatemala, Honduras and El Salvador. They shared some legends and some gods – like Quetzalcoatl – with the Aztecs, but their language and customs were very different.

Nai-mu-ena (say Nahy-moo-ee'-nah) (p. 6-7)
The creator-god of the Colombian Indians.

Obsidian (p. 38)
A dark, glassy rock made from lava.

Quetzal (say ket'-sahl) (p. 25)
The quetzal is a brilliantly coloured bird with green feathers, which lives high up in the tropical rain forest, and is seen only at dawn or dusk. Killing the quetzal was forbidden among the Aztecs, because its feathers were highly prized. The head-dress of Montezuma, the Aztec emperor, included 500 quetzal feathers.

Continued on the next page . . .

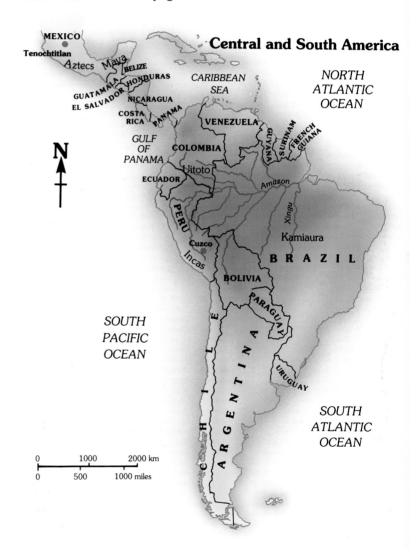

47

Quetzalcoatl (say Ket-sahl-kaw-ah'-tul) (p. 21-5)
The 'Plumed Serpent', half-quetzal and half-rattlesnake, who was the chief god of the Maya and the Aztecs, although Tezcatlipoca also became powerful. Quetzalcoatl was a creator-god, and a god of wind and rain. He is supposed to have given human beings various kinds of knowledge, like how to grow maize and mine gold.

Tenochtitlan (say Ten-ok-teet'-lan) (p. 5)
The main city of the Aztecs. It was a city built on islands in the middle of Lake Texcoco, and was joined to the mainland by long causeways. It had canals for streets, like Venice in Italy, and as many as 200,000 people lived there.

Tepeu (say Tep'-ay-yoo) (p. 32-8)
The Creator. A Mayan god who made the first humans with Gucumatz.

Tezcatlipoca (say Tes-kaht-li-poh'-kah) (p. 21, 24)
Tezcatlipoca, or 'Smoking Mirror', was the most powerful god of the Aztecs. He used his mirror of obsidian to see into the future. Most of the time he was a warlike opponent of Quetzalcoatl, but sometimes they worked together.

Further Reading

The Aztecs, Ancient Peoples and Places series, Richard F. Townsend (Thames and Hudson, 1992)

The Aztecs, Look into the Past series, Peter Hicks (Wayland, 1993)

An Aztec Warrior, Anne Steel (Wayland, 1987)

An Inca Farmer, M. Morrison (Wayland, 1986)

Lost Cities of the Maya, Claude Baudez and Sydney Picasso (Thames and Hudson, 1992)

Mayan Folk Tales, James Sexton (Anchor Press, 1992)

A Mayan Town Through History, edited by Lucilla Watson (Wayland, 1992)

Warriors, Gods and Spirits, D. Gifford (Lowe, 1983)